D1627215

-Read Book

Play Ball

by Margaret Hillert
Illustrated by Dick Martin

DEAR CAREGIVER, The *Beginning-to-Read* series is a carefully written collection of classic readers you may remember from your own childhood. Each book features text comprised of common sight words to provide your child ample practice reading the words that appear most frequently in written text. The many additional details in the pictures enhance the story and offer the opportunity for you to help your child expand oral language and develop comprehension.

Begin by reading the story to your child, followed by letting him or her read familiar words and soon your child will be able to read the story independently. At each step of the way, be sure to praise your reader's efforts to build his or her confidence as an independent reader. Discuss the pictures and encourage your child to make connections between the story and his or her own life. At the end of the story, you will find reading activities and a word list that will help your child practice and strengthen beginning reading skills.

Above all, the most important part of the reading experience is to have fun and enjoy it!

Shannon Cannon

Shannon Cannon,
Literacy Consultant

Norwood House Press • P.O. Box 316598 • Chicago, Illinois 60631
For more information about Norwood House Press please visit our website at *www.norwoodhousepress.com* or call 866-565-2900.

LIBRARY OF CONGRESS CATALOGING-IN-PUBLICATION DATA
Hillert, Margaret.
 Play ball / Margaret Hillert ; illustrated by Dick Martin. — Rev. and expanded library ed.
  p. cm. — (Beginning-to-read series)
 Summary: "Two young boys want to play ball, but they have trouble deciding which game to play"—provided by publisher.
 ISBN-13: 978-1-59953-153-3 (library edition : alk. paper)
 ISBN-10: 1-59953-153-4 (library edition : alk. paper) [1. Balls (Sporting goods)—Fiction.] I. Martin, Dick, 1933– ill. II. Title.
 PZ7.H558Pl 2008
 [E]—dc22   2007035273

Do you want to play ball with me?
We can have fun.
I will run to my house and get a ball.

Now where is that ball?
Where did it go?
I have to find it.

Oh, here it is.
And here is something to go with it.
Now we can play ball.

Oh, no!
Look at you.
I guess we do not want this ball.

But I can get one that we will like.
I will run, run, run.
Do not go away.

No, no.
Get down.
Dogs can not play ball.
We want to play.

Here is the ball I want.
This one will work.
Here I come.

Oh, no!
What do I see now?
What do you have now?

We do not want this ball.
It is not the one for us.
What will we do?

Look, look.
I see something.
Is it a ball?

No, it is not a ball.
We can not play ball with it.
But it can go up.
See it go up.

Help, help!
Look at it go.
Away, away, away.

Oh, oh.
Down we come.
We do not like this.

Come to my house.
I have something that we can play with.
You will see.

Look at that.
I have a ball for that.
I will get it.

See this big ball.
It is fun to play with.
One, two, three.

And ———
UP!

Now you do it.
Do not look down.
Look up, and the ball will go up.

It can go up.
Up, up, and in.
Oh, my.
This is fun.

Jump, jump.
Get it in.
This is the ball for us.

Now we can play ball.
Now we can have fun.

The following activities support the findings of the National Reading Panel that determined the most effective components for reading instruction are: Phonemic Awareness, Phonics, Vocabulary, Fluency, and Text Comprehension.

Phonemic Awareness: Phonograms –all, -ill, -ell

Oral Blending: Say the beginning sounds and word endings below for your child. Ask your child to say the new word made by blending the beginning and ending word parts together:

/b/ + all = ball	/f/ + all = fall	/m/ + all = mall
/h/ + hall = hall	/t/ + all = tall	/w/ + all = wall
/p/ + ill + pill	/h/ + ill = hill	/f/ + ill = fill
/w/ + ill = will	/b/ + ill = bill	/m/ + ill = mill
/s/ + ell = sell	/t/ + ell = tell	/f/ +ell = fell
/y/ + ell = yell	/d/ + ell = dell	/b/ + ell = bell
/sm/ + ell = smell	/gr/ + ill = grill	/sm/ + all = small
/ch/ + ill = chill	/sh/ + ell = shell	/st/ + all = stall

Phonics: Phonograms –all, -ill, -ell

1. Write the following phonograms (word endings) five times each in rows on a piece of paper: _all, _ill, _ell.

2. For each row, help your child write a letter (or letters) in the blank to make a word. If you have letter tiles, or magnetic letters, it may help your child to move the letter into the space.

3. Ask your child to read the rhyming words in each row.

Vocabulary: Opposites

1. The story features the concepts of up and down. Discuss opposites and ask your child to name the opposites of the following:

run (walk)   here (there)   yes (no)   stand (sit)   hot (cold)
buy (sell)   sleep (wake)   over (under)   near (far)   outside (inside)

2. Write each of the words on separate pieces of paper. Mix the words up and ask your child to put the opposite pairs back together.

Fluency: Shared Reading

1. Reread the story to your child at least two more times while your child tracks the print by running a finger under the words as they are read. Ask your child to read the words he or she knows with you.

2. Reread the story taking turns, alternating readers between sentences or pages of the story.

Text Comprehension: Discussion Time

1. Ask your child to retell the sequence of events in the story.

2. To check comprehension, ask your child the following questions:

- Look at page 7. Why can't the boys play ball together?
- What kind of ball did they finally play with together?
- Look at pages 28 and 29. How do you think the boys feel? Why?
- What kind of balls do you like to play with? Do you like to play alone or with a friend? Why?

WORD LIST

***Play Ball* uses the 58 words listed below.** This list can be used to practice reading the words that appear in the text. You may wish to write the words on index cards and use them to help your child build automatic word recognition. Regular practice with these words will enhance your child's fluency in reading connected text.

a	find	jump	red	want
and	for		run	we
at	fun	like		what
away		look	see	where
	get		something	will
ball	go	me		with
big	guess	my	that	work
but			the	
	have	no	this	you
can	help	not	three	
come	here	now	to	
	house		two	
did		oh		
do	I	one	up	
dogs	in		us	
down	is	play		
	it			

ABOUT THE AUTHOR Margaret Hillert has written over 80 books for children who are just learning to read. Her books have been translated into many different languages and over a million children throughout the world have read her books. She first started writing poetry as a child and has continued to write for children and adults throughout her life. A first grade teacher for 34 years, Margaret is now retired from teaching and lives in Michigan where she likes to write, take walks in the morning, and care for her three cats.

Photograph by Glenna Washburn

ABOUT THE ADVISER Shannon Cannon contributed the activities pages that appear in this book. Shannon serves as a literacy consultant and provides staff development to help improve reading instruction. She is a frequent presenter at educational conferences and workshops. Prior to this she worked as an elementary school teacher and as president of a curriculum publishing company.